PUFFIN BOOKS

PIRATE PENGUINS AND THE SARDINES OF DOOM

Frank Rodgers has written and illustrated a wide range of books for children: picture books, story books, non-fiction and novels. His children's stories have been broadcast on radio and TV and a sitcom series based on his book *The Intergalactic Kitchen* was created for CBBC. His recent work for Puffin includes the Eyetooth books, the bestselling Witch's Dog and Robodog titles and now a swashbuckling new series, Pirate Penguins. Frank was an art teacher before becoming an author and illustrator, and he lives in Glasgow with his wife. He has two grown-up children.

Books by Frank Rodgers

For younger readers

PIRATE PENGUINS

PIRATE PENGUINS AND THE
SARDINES OF DOOM

THE WITCH'S DOG

THE WITCH'S DOG AT THE
SCHOOL OF SPELLS

THE WITCH'S DOG AND THE
MAGIC CAKE

THE WITCH'S DOG AND THE
CRYSTAL BALL

THE WITCH'S DOG AND THE
FLYING CARPET

THE WITCH'S DOG AND THE
ICE-CREAM WIZARD

THE WITCH'S DOG AND THE
BOX OF TRICKS

THE WITCH'S DOG AND THE
TALKING PICTURE

THE ROBODOG

THE ROBODOG AND THE BIG DIG

THE ROBODOG, SUPERHERO

THE BUNK-BED BUS

For older readers

EYETOOTH

BATTLE FOR EYETOOTH

Frank Rodgers
Pirate Penguins
and the Sardines
of Doom

PUFFIN

To all polar bears – may the floes be with you

PUFFIN BOOKS

Published by the Penguin Group
Penguin Books Ltd, 80 Strand, London WC2R 0RL, England
Penguin Group (USA) Inc., 375 Hudson Street, New York, New York 10014, USA
Penguin Group (Canada), 90 Eglinton Avenue East, Suite 700, Toronto, Ontario, Canada M4P 2Y3
(a division of Pearson Penguin Canada Inc.)
Penguin Ireland, 25 St Stephen's Green, Dublin 2, Ireland (a division of Penguin Books Ltd)
Penguin Group (Australia), 250 Camberwell Road, Camberwell, Victoria 3124, Australia
(a division of Pearson Australia Group Pty Ltd)
Penguin Books India Pvt Ltd, 11 Community Centre, Panchsheel Park, New Delhi – 110 017, India
Penguin Group (NZ), 67 Apollo Drive, Rosedale, North Shore 0632, New Zealand
(a division of Pearson New Zealand Ltd)
Penguin Books (South Africa) (Pty) Ltd, 24 Sturdee Avenue, Rosebank, Johannesburg 2196, South Africa

Penguin Books Ltd, Registered Offices: 80 Strand, London WC2R 0RL, England

puffinbooks.com

Published 2007
4

Text and illustrations copyright © Frank Rodgers, 2007
All rights reserved

The moral right of the author/illustrator has been asserted

Set in Times New Roman Schoolbook
Made and printed in Singapore by Star Standard

British Library Cataloguing in Publication Data
A CIP catalogue record for this book is available from the British Library

ISBN: 978–0–141–32287–2

Chapter One

The crew of the iceberg ship, the *Frozen Kipper*, were taking it easy.

Paisley, the captain, was trying out a few fancy cutlass swings . . .

Posso, the first mate, was having a
little lie-down . . .

Spott, the lookout,
was polishing
his telescope . . .

and Kelty, the cook, was fishing
for dinner.

"It's nice to have a break," said Paisley. "All that sailing around hunting for treasure can be tiring at times."

Kelty felt a tug on his fishing line.
"Ah," he said. "I've caught something!"

"As long as it's not sardines," said Posso.

3

"What's wrong with sardines?" Spott called down.

"They bring bad luck," answered Posso.

"Around here they're known as *sardines of doom.*"

"Why are they called that?" asked Kelty as he reeled in his catch. "Sardines are nice little fish. Tasty too."

But Posso frowned. "There's an old sailors' saying," he said.

When sardines swim
in the far north sea,
it's doom for you
and it's doom for me.

"Oh dear," said Spott. "I don't like the sound of that."

"Sardines of doom," scoffed Paisley. "Don't be silly. Sardines don't like cold seas. They like the warmer seas of the south. We'll never see them here. Never."

At that moment Kelty hauled his
catch on to the deck.
Everyone stared.

Posso fell
out of his
hammock.

"You've caught sardines!" he gasped.
"We're doomed. Doomed!"
"Nonsense," said Paisley.

But seconds later there was a
tremendous CRACK. Everyone looked
up to see a huge chunk falling off a
nearby iceberg. Down it came . . .

SPLASH!

. . . narrowly missing the
Frozen Kipper.

"Whew! That was close," said Kelty.
"You see, I told you," cried Posso.
"We're doomed . . . and it's all
because of these
silly sardines!"

Chapter Two

Posso quickly gathered up the fish and threw them overboard.

"Oi!" said a voice from below.
"Be careful where you're throwing your sardines!"
Paisley, Posso, Kelty and Spott looked over the side.

A large polar bear sat on a small ice
floe. The sardines had fallen on top
of him.

"Sorry," said Paisley.

"It's all right," sighed the polar
bear. "There are sardines everywhere
these days.
It's not good news."

"What are you doing on that little ice floe?" asked Paisley.

The polar bear sighed again. "My family and I were sitting by our fishing hole trying to catch something apart from sardines. Suddenly the ice broke up into little bits and I was left stranded. It's the sea's fault. It's getting too warm . . . but nobody knows why."

"Where is your family?" Paisley went on.

The polar bear looked sad. "I don't know. We drifted apart and lost each other. I've been looking for them for ages but I haven't got very far on this little floe."
He stood up and stuck out his thumb hopefully. "Any chance of a lift? My name's Minto."

"Of course," said Paisley. "Hop aboard."

As Minto, the polar bear, climbed up on to the deck of the *Frozen Kipper,* Spott gave a shout.

"Ship ahoy on the starboard bow!"

"What kind of ship?" Paisley asked.

"Well . . . it's not exactly a ship," Spott replied, peering more carefully. "It's actually another little ice floe . . . with a big polar bear on it."

"That must be Rona, my wife!" exclaimed Minto in delight. He called up to Spott. "Are the cubs with her?"

"I don't see any," replied Spott.

Minto's face fell. "Oh no," he said. "I wonder what's happened to them?"

"Don't worry," said Paisley. "We'll soon find out."

The *Frozen Kipper* raced over the waves . . .

and, in no time at all, a tearful Rona was clambering aboard.

Minto gave her a big hug.
"The cubs have been
kidnapped, Minto
dear," she wailed.

"We got separated and I saw a
pirate ship come along and take
them. I tried to catch up but I
couldn't."

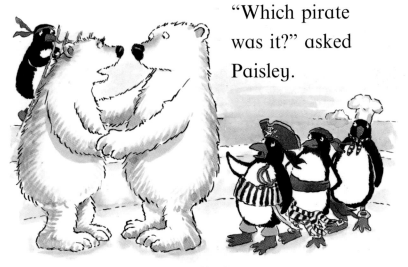

"Which pirate
was it?" asked
Paisley.

"Goldflipper," replied Rona.

"Who's Goldflipper?"
asked Posso.

"He's a big, bad,
bold penguin
buccaneer," said
Minto with a
frown.

"So am I," said
Paisley, "in case
you haven't noticed."

"And so are we,"
added Posso,
Spott and Kelty
quickly.

"But I mean *really* big and *really* bad,"
replied Minto.

"He doesn't scare me," said Paisley.

"Er . . . or us," added Posso, Spott and Kelty.

"I heard one of his crew shout that they were going to Snowball Mountain," Rona said.

"Then that's where we're going," said Paisley. "We'll show them who are the biggest and boldest pirates around here. We'll get your cubs back, Rona. Don't worry."

"Oh, thank you!" cried Rona.
"Thank you!"

"But what about your ship?" said
Minto. "Aren't you afraid it'll fall to
bits like the other icebergs?"

"That's a chance we'll have to take,"
said Paisley.

"You're so brave!"
cried Rona, giving
Paisley a big
kiss on the
cheek.

Paisley blushed
bright red.

"What are you lot grinning at?" he
said gruffly as smiles spread on the
faces of his crew. "Look lively there!
Jump to it and set a course for
Snowball Mountain!"

Chapter Three

As the *Frozen Kipper* sailed north, icebergs fell to bits all around it.

Paisley and the crew, helped by Minto and Rona, rushed around the ship mending cracks and making sure parts didn't fall off. It was tiring work.

But at last, to everyone's relief,
Spott yelled, "Land ahoy!
Snowball Mountain!"

Up ahead the huge ball of snow on
top of Snowball Mountain glistened
in the bright air. Around it the sky
was red and flickered strangely.
Clouds of steam rose into the sky.

The *Frozen Kipper* sailed into a quiet
bay and dropped anchor. Paisley
and the others rowed ashore and
clambered quickly up the hillside.
Stealthily, they peered over the top.

Down below on the seashore were
the remains of an
ancient castle.

On its battlements stood a row of
enormous, steaming cauldrons. Huge
fires were burning underneath them,
stoked by Goldflipper's pirates.
"Whew! I can feel the heat from here,"
whispered Spott, wiping his brow.

"Those cauldrons were once used for throwing hot oil over the castle's attackers," said Paisley.
"Not very nice," said Posso.

"But they're not full of oil now," Paisley went on. "They're full of hot water!"

As they watched, the pirates turned great handles and the cauldrons tipped over. Hot, steaming water poured into the sea. Immediately the cauldrons were filled up again.

"That's the reason the sea's getting warmer," said Paisley. "But why are they doing it?"

"To attract the sardines," Minto said.
"Goldflipper loves sardines but he
knows that these waters are too cold
for them.

By making the sea warmer Goldflipper
has tricked the sardines into swimming
here so he can catch them."
"But he's ruining everything," protested
Kelty. "Soon there'll be no ice left."

"He doesn't care," said Minto.
"As long as he gets his sardines
he's happy."

"The sardines of doom," said
Posso glumly.
Suddenly, Rona gasped. "There!" she
cried, pointing.

Everyone looked. In the far corner
of the courtyard were three polar
bear cubs, guarded by a bunch of
nasty-looking pirates.

"The children!" exclaimed Minto and
his bushy brows furrowed angrily.
"If Goldflipper has harmed one hair
on their little faces, I'll . . ."

Minto began to get to his feet but
Paisley pulled him back down.
"Take it easy,"
whispered
Paisley.

"There are too many of them. We
need a rescue plan. Let's get closer
and find out what's happening."
Stealthily, he began to crawl down
the hill.

Chapter Four

Moving silently, they reached the outer wall of the castle and peered carefully into the courtyard.

In one corner was a blacksmith's forge. In front of it stood a large treasure chest. Goldflipper had dug it up on Snowball Mountain.

The three young polar bears were
being made to work hard.

Watched by the guards, they were
taking big piles of shimmering gold
coins from the chest into the forge.

"The poor things,"
whispered Rona.

From inside the forge came the
roaring of a fire and the clanging
of hammers.

"What are they
doing with the
gold coins?"
wondered Kelty.

Just then out of the forge came a
pirate trundling a wheelbarrow.

Piled high on the wheelbarrow were
sardine cans . . .

gold sardine cans!

Paisley gasped.

"They're melting down the gold to make cans," he said.

"Goldflipper must be putting the sardines in them."

33

At that moment an enormous
penguin appeared.

He had a golden hat, a golden eye-
patch, a golden cutlass and a flipper
with a golden hook on the end.

"Guess who," whispered Minto to the others.

"He's certainly big," said Spott.

"And nasty-looking," said Posso.

"He doesn't scare me," said Paisley.

"Er . . . or us, of course," said Posso, Kelty and Spott.

Goldflipper let out a great laugh,
picked up a gold sardine can and
kissed it.

"Gold and sardines
together!" he cried.
"The perfect kind
of treasure. Tasty
and worth a
fortune.

I'm the smartest pirate ever!"

Paisley glared at him. "We'll see
about that," he muttered.

"Does that mean you've thought of
a rescue plan, Paisley?" asked Rona.

Paisley grinned slowly. "Yes," he replied, pointing to the old bell. "That bell has given me an idea. Not only will I rescue the cubs . . .

but I'll defeat Goldflipper and cool the sea down as well."

"But how?" Posso asked.

"Well," said Paisley, "first of all, I'm going to challenge Goldflipper to a duel."

"What?" cried his companions. "You cannot be serious. He'll make mincemeat out of you!"

Paisley smiled. "I don't think so," he said and winked. "Let's get back to the ship and I'll tell you all my plan . . ."

Chapter Five

Half an hour later, Paisley stood
alone in front of the castle. He
waved his cutlass in the air as guards
appeared on the battlements.

"Where's Goldflipper?" Paisley shouted.

The guards were pushed aside and
Goldflipper stood there, staring
down at him.

"Who are you
and what do
you want?" he
demanded.

"I'm a big, bad, bold buccaneer
and I challenge you to a duel,"
cried Paisley. "Come out
and fight if
you dare."

"You? Challenge me?" said Goldflipper. He roared with laughter.  "I'm the biggest, baddest, boldest pirate there is. I'll make mincemeat out of you."

 "I don't think so," replied Paisley.

"Ha! We'll soon see about that," said Goldflipper and charged down the steps towards the door.

Goldflipper's entire pirate crew
crowded on to the battlements, eager
to watch.
This was exactly what Paisley had
been hoping for. Now there was no
one to guard the prisoners.

A moment later, Goldflipper came
out. Close-up he was *huge*.

"So . . ." he said
mockingly as he
stamped towards
Paisley.

"You think you can get the better
of me, do you?"

Paisley bravely stood his ground. "I know I can," he said.

Goldflipper swung his cutlass but Paisley jumped out of the way.

"So do it," said Goldflipper and roared with laughter again.

"All right," said Paisley. From his sash he pulled out the ship's bell.

Holding it up, he rang it as loudly as he could.

Goldflipper snorted. "What are you trying to do?" he sneered.

"Hurt my ears?"

"It's a signal," replied Paisley.

Goldflipper stopped in his tracks. "A signal?" he said warily. "A signal for what?"

Just then there was a loud bang
followed by a crash from the other
side of the castle courtyard.

"For that,"
replied Paisley.

Goldflipper stared up at the
battlements. "What's going on?" he
roared at his crew.

"Two polar bears have just knocked
down the back door," replied one.
"The prisoners are escaping!"

"And a ship has just fired its cannon
at the top of Snowball Mountain,"
cried another. "The giant snowball
has been knocked off . . . *and it's
rolling this way!*"

Chapter Six

It was Paisley's turn to laugh. His plan had worked out perfectly. Posso, Kelty and Spott had aimed the cannon of the *Frozen Kipper* just right . . .

while big, strong Minto and Rona
had easily knocked down the castle's
old back door and rescued their cubs.

Goldflipper ran back up to the
battlements, beside his crew.
He stared in dismay.
Rumbling towards
them was an
enormous snowball . . .
getting bigger and
bigger as it rolled.

"Abandon the
castle!" yelled
Goldflipper in panic.

He and his crew raced out of the
castle and on to their ship.

As they set sail, the gigantic snowball
arrived with a thunderous roar.
The castle and the treasure were
completely covered in snow. With a
great hissing and spluttering the
bonfires went out and the melting
snow poured into the sea, quickly
cooling it down.

Paisley, Minto, Rona and the
rescued cubs were now safely aboard
the *Frozen Kipper*. They all watched
in delight.

"Hooray!" they shouted.

Then their faces fell. Goldflipper's ship was heading straight towards them, its cannons at the ready.

Goldflipper stood on the deck, bristling with anger. He raised his cutlass.

"Take aim!" He shouted to his crew. "Ready . . . *fire!*"

But at that moment a big chunk fell
off a nearby iceberg and crashed
right through the deck . . .

Goldflipper and his crew barely
managed to scramble into a rowing
boat before their ship went down.

"Serves him right," said Paisley as Goldflipper and his pirates rowed away furiously.

"That's the last we'll see of him for a while," he said with a grin.

"And that's the last we'll see of the sardines of doom," Posso said with relief. "Look, they're going home . . . they're swimming south!"

"We're glad they're going too," said Minto. "My family and I don't like sardines."

"But we love big, bad, bold buccaneers," said Rona. And before any of the pirate penguins could get out of the way, she gave them all a big farewell kiss.

This time, Spott, Kelty and Posso turned bright red too.

Chapter Seven

"Things are back to normal now, thank goodness," said Paisley after the polar bears had gone ashore. "The icebergs have stopped falling apart."

Posso yawned and stretched. "Now I can get back to my nice, comfy hammock," he said.

58

"Not yet," said Paisley with a smile.
"There are still some sardines of
doom to be dealt with."

"What do you
mean?" asked
Posso, startled.

Paisley went to the ship's store and
returned with four shovels.

Kelty smiled. "He means that there's
a big pile of gold sardine cans just
waiting to be dug up."

59

"Exactly," said Paisley with a grin.
"So come on, you big, bad, bold,
blushing buccaneers . . .

it's time to go hunting for
treasure again!"